LUCAS LIGHTFOOT and the FIRE CRYSTAL

By Hugo Haselhuhn
with Luke Cowdell

Illustrated by Heather Cowdell

1

LUCAS LIGHTFOOT AND THE FIRE CRYSTAL

ISBN 978-0-9912439-0-7

Acknowledgements

First and foremost, I want to thank my grandson, Luke Cowdell, for having the desire to write a "chapter book" and secondly his mother, Heather Cowdell, for having the audacity to encourage her son to accomplish his dreams. When Luke told his mother of his desire, she assured him that "grandpa" could help him. Many of the ideas and accomplishments of the hero in our story are from the mind of Luke. He told me about the hero and I provided the road, created the characters and painted the scenery along the road they traveled.

I am thankful to my daughter Heather, who is the artistic talent behind the illustrations to help bring the story to life through pictures. I am thankful to Laurel Palmer who captured the essence of the story in the cover art.

I appreciate the input from two special school teachers, Nicole Delbar, who provided insight early in the writing, and, Janice Paxman, who provided careful editing for a polished manuscript. I am also grateful to all of the children and adults who read the early manuscript and provided encouragement and feedback. As one young reader said, "I give it 6 out of 5 stars!"

A special thanks to my wife Lydia, who encouraged me throughout the writing and reminded me that the readers will be children and to write for them. I trusted her with a red pen in her hand and she proved invaluable in editing the story.

Cover art © 2013 Laurel Palmer

The text type is 12-pt. Maiandra GD

Cover Layout Design by Heather Cowdell

Epigrams are quotes selected from the
Book of Prescottian Wisdom

CONTENTS

ONE

LUCAS MEETS PRESCOTT

We might meet by chance, but we are friends by choice.

Lucas slammed on his brakes and skidded to a stop as he swerved his bike off the sidewalk and onto the grass. "What was that?" he asked his dad. "It moved!" Lucas pointed to what he thought was a green stick just inches away from the black skid mark. Whatever it was, it turned its head and looked right at Lucas. He had narrowly missed a small lizard whose tiny scales reflected in the sunlight like emerald dust and ruby tattoos. It was definitely the strangest creature he had ever seen.

Lucas's dad carefully picked up the reptile. "It looks like a lizard," he said. "In fact, I think it is a chameleon. Although this is strange, I have never seen a chameleon wearing a collar. It must belong to someone, but the collar doesn't have a name, just these strange symbols."

"Can we keep it Dad?" asked Lucas.

"Let's take it in the house and keep it safe. Before we decide whether or not to keep it, we need to see if it belongs to one of the neighbors." Lucas knew that they should check with the neighbors, but he hoped that they would not find the owner. After all, who would let such a beautiful creature escape?

Once the chameleon was settled in a cardboard box in Lucas's room, Lucas and his dad walked the neighborhood showing a picture of the chameleon at every door. After they got to the end of the block, they decided that the lizard probably had not gone that far so they crossed the street and walked on the other side. With still no success, they crossed back to their side of the street. After a few houses, Lucas walked up to a house with a rocking horse on the porch and rang the doorbell and prayed that no one was home.

A tall woman answered the door. She had silver hair, deep green eyes, and a very kind face. Lucas thought he saw a hint of recognition in her face and wondered if he had seen her somewhere before. She had a glow about her when she smiled and asked, "Can I help you?"

"Did you lose a chameleon?" Lucas asked holding up a photograph of the green creature.

The woman's eyes lit up. "Where did you find him?" she asked.

Lucas related the story of the near miss on the sidewalk in front of his house and explained that they had him safe at home.

"My name is Katrina," the woman said, "and the chameleon belonged to my son, but it had escaped from his cage over a year ago. I'm very surprised that it is still alive."

"Two years ago, my son had been given the chameleon by a friend who owed him some money," the woman explained. "Supposedly, it was a magic lizard worth far more than the $500 owed him. My son did not expect to ever get his money back so he took the chameleon, never once believing the claim that it was magical."

"My son didn't believe that there was any magic in that chameleon, but now I'm not so sure." And then with a smile she said, "How could he live on his own for so long if he didn't have a little magic in him?"

"I'm glad we found you," said Lucas's dad. "We'll go get the chameleon and bring him right back." Lucas had hoped to keep the chameleon, but now he would have to give it back.

"Oh no! My son has moved to the east coast, and I no longer have the cage. Would you be willing to give the chameleon a good home and take really good care of him?"

Lucas's face split into a big grin. "Please! Please, Dad! Can I keep him?"

"Well, we will have to get your mother to agree, but leave that to me, I think I can work a little magic of my own."

"Before you go, I think I still have a few books on caring for chameleons. Would you like them?"

"Sure!" said Lucas and his dad together.

While she was gone, Lucas said, "We should give the chameleon a name."

"I agree. Since you found him you should choose. What name would you like?"

Lucas thought for a while. "It needs to be a good name because this is a very special chameleon, maybe even magical. Lizards like to warm themselves in the sun so maybe a name that is warm. I was doing some homework this week and came across a town called Prescott, Arizona. Since Prescott is a warm town, I think I will call him Prescott."

"That will be a fine name for a good looking lizard," said his dad.

The woman returned and handed two books to Lucas. "Be sure to read about the care and feeding of chameleons because they are not native to North America," she said. "Most chameleons come from Africa or Madagascar, and this particular breed lives in the forest. He likes trees, leaves, and branches."

They thanked the woman again, and as they turned to go she said, "I wish you luck understanding the symbols on the collar. It may be that you will find the magic in those symbols. I forgot to tell you, Lucas, the chameleon's name is Prescott, but since he is yours now, you can name him anything you like."

Lucas and his dad turned to look at each other with a wide-eyed look of amazement, then back at the woman who just smiled, waved and retreated inside the house and closed the door.

"Wow! Did you hear that?" said Lucas. "It's as if she could read my mind."

Lucas and his dad ran home to share the news. And silently, Lucas determined that he was going to find the magic in Prescott.

That afternoon, after reading some of the basics about caring for a chameleon, Lucas and his family went to the local pet store. Lucas read that chameleons love crickets. When a chameleon is on the hunt it may sit quietly and wait for prey to come near, or it may move slowly and quietly along a branch or the ground. It has funny mitten-like feet to give it a firm grip on a branch and its two eyes turn in different directions at once, looking for the slightest movement for food. No other animal on Earth has eyes and feet like these!

They bought a cage with a lamp and some crickets for Prescott. Since lizards are cold-blooded, they need the heat from the sun or a light to keep them warm. They decorated Prescott's new home with some branches and leaves from a tree in the yard and a flat bowl for water. They released five crickets into the cage and watched Prescott to see what he would do. Lucas had read that when a chameleon spots an insect or other prey, its eyes lock in on the target. After taking careful aim, the chameleon shoots out its super-long tongue which is usually longer than its body. The tip of the tongue is wet and shaped like a suction cup. So when it smacks against the prey, it sticks tight and the tongue then slips back into the chameleon's open mouth. Everyone was watching closely to see if Prescott was hungry. They did not have to wait very long. At first, Prescott waited very still until a cricket came close, and then his tongue shot out of his mouth and the cricket became dinner in less than a second. Lucas's little sister squealed with delight and clapped her hands when she saw the long tongue shoot out and the cricket disappear into Prescott's mouth. Within a short time, all of the crickets were gone and Prescott looked at Lucas as if to say,

"Thank you. I was very hungry."

That night, the cage for Prescott was set up in Lucas's room near

his bed. He had had a very exciting day. He almost ran over a chameleon, and now the chameleon was his pet, a gift from Katrina. As he thought about the woman that gave him Prescott, Lucas remembered where he had seen her. She was in a dream he had had several nights ago. He didn't remember much about the dream except for her kind face, soft voice and her beautiful green eyes. It just occurred to him that as he and his dad were leaving her house, she called him Lucas, but he had not told her his name. Just thinking about that gave him goose bumps and he pulled the covers up to his neck to keep warm. Lucas drifted off to sleep thinking about Prescott, but little did he know that finding Prescott would change his life in ways he could never imagine. To those that did not know Lucas Lightfoot, he appeared to be an average boy from an average family living in Southern California, but that had all changed today. Yes, it will be a day long remembered as the day Lucas met Prescott.

TWO

SURPRISE AWAKENING

Allow yourself a few surprises everyday and enjoy the wonders around you.

The first thing Lucas did when he woke up the next morning was to go over to Prescott and say,

"Good morning."

As he got close to the cage, Prescott turned both eyes toward Lucas, winked and stuck out his tongue just a little and wiggled it. Lucas thought that was really weird as if Prescott was saying good morning to him. At that moment, Lucas remembered the strange dream he had had and he went into his parents' room.

"I had a really strange dream last night. I dreamed that Prescott called me by my name, and thanked me for saving his life, giving him a nice warm home, and providing delicious crickets to eat. Isn't that funny?"

"Yesterday was definitely exciting," his mother said, "I am sure that is what caused your dream."

Lucas agreed and went back to his room and pulled out the books he had received from his neighbor. As he looked through the books, he saw that there were a lot more varieties of chameleons than he had thought.

Lucas had once heard that chameleons change colors to match their surroundings. He read that chameleons hang out where their normal, 'everyday' colors match their surroundings. In other words, a normally green chameleon usually lives among green leaves, and brown ones may live on the ground. This helps hide them from predators and makes it easier for them to surprise their prey.

Chameleons may turn lighter to cool down or darker to warm up because dark colors take in more heat from the sun. Chameleons may also change color when they become frightened, angry, or feel stressed.

Lucas smiled when he remembered that his Grandpa Jack sometimes turns red in the face when he gets stressed. He read on to learn that chameleons use their colors to communicate with one another.

One color may mean, "Stay away from me!"

A different color may mean, "Do you want to be my friend?"

As Lucas was reading through the book and looking at the different colors and species of chameleons, he decided that Prescott was the most beautiful type. When he got to the end of the book, he found a small envelope taped to the inside back cover. He opened the envelope and found a thin disk inside. The disk was about two and half inches in diameter and about one sixteenth inch thick. It was cool to the touch like some kind of metal. The disk appeared to be two pieces: an inner flat disk and an outer ring that was raised slightly. The inner disk was red with a hole in the middle and it had a small triangle-like pointer. The outer ring was green and was able to spin around the inner disk but both the pieces were locked together. The outer ring was divided into eight sections with a line dividing the sections. In each of the sections was a strange symbol that Lucas had never seen. But wait, he HAD seen these before. They were the same symbols that were on Prescott's collar.

He turned over the disk to look at the backside and saw the following inscription in a circular shape around the outer ring:

VIRTUE UNLOCKS POWER

Lucas was not certain about the meaning of VIRTUE, so he decided to look it up. There were several definitions, but which one was the right one for this disk?

Virtue:
1. *Conformity to a standard of right or particular moral excellence*
2. *Quality or power of a thing*
3. *Manly strength or courage*

Lucas decided that he should go ask his mother and he found her in the kitchen.

"Mom, I have a question. What does virtue mean?"

"Well, it means to have high morals or honorable standards. Do you remember how we've talked about making good decisions and choosing between right and wrong? If you make the right choice, then you are showing others that you have high moral standards or virtue."

Lucas thought about that for a little bit and then asked,

"How does virtue unlock power?"

His mother was a little surprised that her ten-year-old son was asking such grown-up questions.

"What exactly do you mean? Where are you getting these questions?"

Lucas was concerned that the disk he found in the back of the book might be valuable, and he might have to return it to the woman. However, she seemed pretty insistent that Lucas take Prescott, and she DID give him the book. He decided to let his mom in on his discovery.

Lucas said, "Let me show you something."

Lucas reached into his pocket and pulled out the red and green disk and handed it to his mother.

"I found this in the back of one of the books the woman gave me. It looks like it may be

21

expensive. The markings on the front are the same as on Prescott's collar, and the outer ring spins around the inside. But what's really strange is the writing on the back."

Lucas's mother turned over the disk and read the words slowly turning the disk as she read.

"VIRTUE UNLOCKS POWER."

"You are right," his mother said, "It is very strange. I wonder if the woman that gave you Prescott knew about this disk. You and your dad should probably go ask the woman about this and see if she can tell you what it is."

Lucas agreed thinking that Katrina could tell him if the magic was in the ring. Lucas showed his father the disk and he agreed that they should talk with the woman again. Lucas and his father walked up to the house with the rocking horse on the porch. They knocked on the door and heard the sound of little feet running toward the door. A young woman opened the door and there were two little girls standing beside her.

"Yes, can I help you?" asked the woman.

Lucas's father asked, "Is Katrina here?"

"I am sorry. There is no Katrina who lives here," said the young mother.

Lucas and his father looked at each other very confused.

"We were here last Saturday afternoon and spoke with a woman named Katrina who had lost a chameleon that my son found. She had silver hair and green eyes," said Lucas's father.

"Oh, you must be thinking of Katherine. She sold us this home about a year ago. We were gone all weekend and I cannot imagine that she could have talked with you. She moved to a senior care home and is confined to a wheelchair," explained the young mother.

Not wanting to try to explain how they met Katrina as she stood in this house while the owners were gone, Lucas's father said,

"I guess we made a mistake. Thank you for the information. By the way, my name is Andrew and this is my son Lucas and we live five houses up the street."

"It's nice to meet you. And I'm sorry I couldn't be of more help," said the woman.

Lucas had a lot more questions than answers as they walked home. "I guess that means I can keep the 'Power Ring' since there is no one to return it to."

His father agreed and said, "With Katrina gone, I guess we will never know what the symbols on the ring mean."

For the next few nights Lucas dreamed that Prescott was talking to him, but it seemed maybe more like Lucas was able to hear Prescott's thoughts. He dreamed that Prescott was telling him about the symbols on the Power Ring.

"One symbol represents the power to stop time, another, the power to be invisible to others, and another the power of telekinesis."

In his dream, Lucas had the thought to ask Prescott about the purpose of the other symbols.

Prescott said, *"The purpose of the other symbols will be revealed if you meet the challenges ahead."*

Still dreaming, Lucas "heard" Prescott say, *"Do you think that finding me on the sidewalk was by chance? Do you think that speaking with Katrina was also by some coincidence? No, Lucas. I chose you because you are someone very special. I want to teach you about the power of the ring because you have a good heart. But remember, Lucas, this power can only be used for good and*

for unselfish reasons. If you try to use this power to control others or for personal gain, it simply will not work! Or it may work in unexpected ways, so be careful. Remember, you must serve others. With this power comes the responsibility to use it wisely and it can only be used with virtue."

Lucas bolted awake and jumped out of bed. He noticed that it was still dark outside and the red numbers on the clock indicated that it was 3:45 in the morning. Lucas turned on the small desk lamp, lifted the cover on the cage, and looked at Prescott. Prescott was looking directly at Lucas.

Lucas quietly said, "I was having a dream that you were talking to me." No sooner were the words out of his mouth, than Lucas heard a voice in his head.

"I was talking with you! I was telling you all about the Power Ring and some of the symbols."

Lucas fell back on the bed, rubbed his eyes, and then pinched himself to make sure he was not still dreaming. In his head he heard Prescott's voice again.

"Lucas, my name is Prescott. You can pinch yourself all you want, but you are most definitely awake and we have a lot to talk about."

THREE

THE POWER RING

Give someone adversity to test his strength.
Give him power to test his character.

For the rest of the night, Prescott told
Lucas the history behind the Power Ring and how
Prescott became the guardian. Lucas listened to
Prescott's voice inside his head as if they were his
own thoughts. And when Lucas had a question,
all he had to do was think about it.

Prescott began, *"Lucas, I have been*
watching you for some time. When I determined
that my last caretaker was undeserving of the ring,
I began looking for someone who would value
this gift and be worthy of its power. I have seen
how you treat your family and friends and even
those who are unkind to you. When I crawled on
to the sidewalk in front of your bicycle, I knew
you would stop. I am sure that you would like to

*know a little about me and how a talking
chameleon came into your life. You might be
surprised to know that I am almost one hundred
years old. My original home was in the rain forest
in Madagascar. My keeper was a shaman.*"

Lucas interrupted, "What is a shaman?"

"*A shaman is a very wise man. He taught
me the skills I will now teach you. He fashioned
the Power Ring you found and gave it power from
the crystal in the center.*"

Lucas interrupted and said, "But there is no
crystal in the center of the ring."

Prescott replied, "*Very clever. You did
notice that the crystal is indeed missing, and I will
need your help to replace it.*"

"*The Power Ring operates by the power of
your virtue or goodness, and by the power within
crystal. You turn the pointer on the center disk
toward the desired power and squeeze the disk.
The crystal that fits into the center ring is a Fire
Crystal and looks like a ruby. It was found near
my home in Madagascar and cut by the shaman.*"

There is natural frequency within the structure of the crystal at which it vibrates, and when combined with virtue and your positive thoughts, power is generated. The energy from the crystal will boost your will power, courage, and inner strength. It has a powerful positive quality and will magnify your positive thoughts. The power, however is cancelled by negative thoughts."

Prescott continued his thoughts in Lucas's head.

"As you use the power ring and develop a connection to it, you will find that you no longer need to turn the pointer or squeeze the ring. You will develop the power of telekinesis and you can move it with your mind."

Lucas interrupted again and asked,

"What is te-le-ki-ne-sis?"

"Telekinesis is the power to move objects by just the power of your thought and is just one of the powers I will teach you."

"Does each symbol represent some power?" asked Lucas.

"Yes," replied Prescott. *"I will tell you about three of the symbols and the power linked to each to start your training. The first power you may use is telekinesis. At first you will be able to move small items like pencils or toys. The symbol is the Three Arrows pointing right to remind you to do what's right."*

Prescott continued, *"The second power will be the ability to stop time. That power is represented by the Double-T with the Sun above. You may use this to protect someone from injury."*

"With the third power, you will be able to become invisible. That is the symbol that looks like a Double-S."

"Cool'" thought Lucas, *"I will be able to hide from mom and dad and play tricks on my little sister."*

Lucas heard Prescott in his mind, *"These powers are not to be used foolishly."*

Lucas replied in a whisper, "Oops! I forgot you can hear me think."

Lucas did not remember going back to sleep but he jumped out of bed when the alarm went off.

He looked over at Prescott and thought, *"Was I dreaming?"*

Immediately he heard Prescott's voice in his head, *"You were not dreaming, and you need to keep our secret to yourself until the time is right to tell others."*

Lucas agreed and went off to get ready for school.

Lucas was sitting at his desk in class, deep in thought about the conversations with Prescott and about the Power Ring.

"Lucas. Lucas!"

He snapped out of his day-dreaming and said, "Yes, Prescott."

His teacher said, "That's a good guess, but the capital of Arizona is Phoenix."

Some of the other children were giggling but Kevin, the class bully, was laughing the hardest. This really bothered Lucas, and he wished he could use some of the powers to teach Kevin a lesson. He remembered that the Power Ring can only be used for good so he let it go. Lucas did not like Kevin and tried to stay out of his way. Kevin was bigger than all of the other kids and he used that to his advantage.

Lauren Harrison, Lucas's teacher, was young and pretty and Lucas liked her. She made school fun, but sitting next to Hailey made school so much better! Hailey had blond hair and blue eyes and dimples in her cheeks when she smiled. Lucas liked Hailey and thought that there was something special about her. Lucas wanted to share his secret with her, but he knew he needed to wait as Prescott instructed him. Besides, she might think he was weird talking about a magical chameleon. Lucas had a feeling that someday he would be able to share his secret with Hailey.

FOUR

THE FIRE CRYSTAL

The road ahead is best traveled when our companion is one we trust.

When Lucas got home from school, he went to his room to check on Prescott. He was sitting very still on a branch with his back to Lucas. Without turning his head, Prescott opened his eyes and rotated them backward to look at Lucas and said,

"So you think I have funny eyes."

"Oops," said Lucas, "I keep forgetting you can hear my thoughts."

"That's okay," said Prescott, *"Because I am different, that makes me special and unique."*

Lucas's mother called from the hall, "Lucas, who are you talking to?"

Lucas replied, "I'm just talking to Prescott."

"I guess that is okay as long as he doesn't talk back to you."

"Really, Mom?" said Lucas, "A talking chameleon?"

His mom asked, "What did you mean when you said, 'I keep forgetting you can hear my thoughts'"?

Lucas heard Prescott in his head, *"Just tell your mother that you are playing an imaginary game with me, and ask your mother if she can make a special shoulder pack so you can carry me. I have a special task for you and I need you to take me somewhere."*

"Oh, you heard that?" said Lucas to his mom. "I was just playing an imaginary game with

Prescott. Mom, can you make a shoulder pack so I can carry Prescott with me?"

"He wants me.... I mean, um, I want to take him with me sometimes when I go out."

Lucas's mother thought this behavior was a little strange but decided to play along and asked, "What kind of pack do you want?"

Lucas could hear Prescott in his thoughts, *"Like Uncle Brett's."*

"Well, maybe you could make it something like the one-shoulder pack that Uncle Brett has," said Lucas.

"Make the outer covering with mesh so I can breathe."

"And Mom, can you make the outer covering with mesh so I can... I mean so Prescott can breathe," said Lucas in response to his prompting.

"Make it green so I cannot be easily seen."

"And can you make it green like Prescott so he can be like a chameleon and be hidden? That way people won't know that I have him."

That night Lucas asked if he could go to bed early. He didn't tell his mother that he was up half the night listening to a chameleon because she might think that he was taking this imaginary game too far.

Again in the middle of the night, Lucas heard Prescott invading his sleep.

"Lucas. Lucas, wake up! I need you to hear what I have to say. I heard your thoughts at dinner when your mother asked about your day. I know that you wanted to say what you would like to do to Kevin, but the power can only be used for good."

"Yes, I know," said Lucas sleepily, "Did you wake me to tell me that?"

"That and more. I need you to take me to where I have hidden the Fire Crystal. We can go after school to get it," said Prescott.

"But you said it was in the creek," said Lucas, "and my mom doesn't want me to go to the creek."

"Leave your mom to me," said Prescott. "Just come home right after school. Now go back to sleep."

The next day Lucas came right home from school and was just getting ready to ask his mom if he could take Prescott to the creek when she asked him a question.

"Lucas, can you do me a favor? Your brother kicked his ball over the fence and into the creek behind the house. Can you go up the street to the footpath bridge and go down into the creek and get the ball?"

It hadn't rained for over a month so she knew there would be very little water in the creek.

Lucas was surprised that his mom would ask him to go to the creek and then he remembered that Prescott said "he would take care of his mom."

Lucas asked, "Can I take Prescott with me?"

"Why do you want to do that?" replied his mom.

"I need him for protection." Lucas had no idea why he said that or why he would need protection.

His mom replied, playing along with what she thought was his imaginary game,

"Sure, if you think you need protection, but please be careful with him." His mom then said, "I made the shoulder pack you requested. It's on the kitchen table."

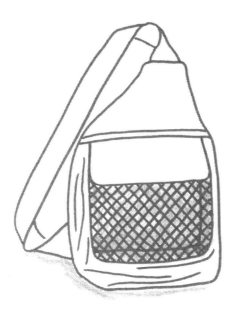

Lucas thanked his mom with a kiss, grabbed the pack, and ran to get Prescott. As he was taking him out of the cage, Lucas asked, "Did you do that?"

"Of course I did. I told you we needed to do something important. Do you have the Power Ring?"

"It's in my pocket," replied Lucas.

"Good. We need to go now."

Lucas put Prescott in the shoulder pack and slipped it over his head. He walked toward the bridge at the end of the court with Prescott riding in the pack across his chest. What Lucas did not know is that Kevin lived on the other side of the creek near the bridge. Kevin saw Lucas go down into the creek bed and thought he would have some fun with Lucas.

Prescott was in Lucas's head again, *"After you get to the creek, get the ball, throw it back to your mom, and then you need to find the crystal for the ring."*

Lucas did as instructed. He found the ball and threw it back over the fence.

His mom said, "Thank you. See you back at the house."

Prescott said, "*Lucas, I want you to go back to the bridge and find a triangular rock by the cement wall. Under the rock you will find a small metal box and in the box is the fire crystal.*"

Lucas did not see that he was being watched as he went under the bridge.

Lucas found the rock and tried to lift it but it would not budge. "It is too heavy," said Lucas.

"*Let me try,*" said Prescott.

41

Lucas watched as the rock slowly slid to the side to reveal a golden box with strange designs engraved on the surface. Lucas reached into the cavity and lifted the golden box and set it on his lap. He slowly opened the box to reveal a red crystal that was a little smaller than a dime.

"Lucas, hold the crystal over the center of the Power Ring."

As he did, he heard Prescott say something in a language he had never heard and the crystal slipped from his fingers. It felt like the crystal was being pulled into the ring like two magnets. The Power Ring started vibrating and getting warmer.

"Turn the outer ring so that the arrow is pointing to the symbol that is a Double-S," said Prescott, with some urgency in his voice. *"And now squeeze that*

symbol quickly, someone is coming."

"You need to trust me," said Prescott, "Be very still and you will be invisible to others."

A few seconds later, Lucas heard someone coming down the bank to the creek. Kevin Cherno came around the corner of the cement wall with a plastic bag. Lucas's heart started pounding as he held his breath.

Lucas heard Prescott say, "So this is the Kevin in your class? You do not need to fear. To him you are invisible."

Lucas was still scared. He looked behind him to see if he could run that way, but his escape was blocked by overgrown bushes. He could make a run for it across the creek but he would get his shoes and pants wet. There was no going forward since Kevin was blocking any escape in that direction. Lucas decided that he would have to trust Prescott so he sat very still.

Kevin was scanning the area under the bridge looking for rocks that Lucas could hide behind.

"Hey Lucas," Kevin called out almost snarling as he talked, "Come on out, I have a surprise for you."

"Lucas," said Prescott in a very soft and calm voice and knowing exactly what he was thinking, *"even though you can see yourself and me, he cannot see us."*

Sure enough, Kevin looked directly at Lucas but did not show any signs of recognition.

"Lucas, I know you are down here. I saw you come down to get that ball. Come out, come out, wherever you are."

Lucas sat very still as Kevin walked closer to where he and Prescott were sitting. His heart was pounding so hard he could hear the thumping in his own ears. Kevin came within a few feet of where Lucas was sitting on the rock as he continued to look for places where he thought Lucas might be hiding.

He heard Kevin mumble, "I guess that little twerp snuck out the other side. Too bad he missed the surprise I had for him."

Kevin reached into the plastic bag and pulled out a water balloon and threw it against the cement wall across the creek. It hit the wall with a splash. He pulled out another and threw it at a large rock near Lucas and a little of the water splashed on him.

"Do you want to see how the power of telekinesis works?" asked Prescott.

Without saying a word, Lucas just nodded his head.

Kevin pulled out another balloon and threw it on the wall nearby. He was totally surprised when the water balloon didn't pop as expected, but instead bounced off of the wall and came right back at him and broke against his belt buckle soaking him from his waist down.

"What the heck! How was that possible? It should have broken on the wall!"

Angrily Kevin pulled out the last balloon and just as he was throwing it overhand the balloon exploded above his head drenching him.

"Aaahh!" screamed Kevin.

Lucas could not help himself from giggling and Kevin spun around and looked right in Lucas's direction but made no movement toward him. Kevin turned back toward to the open end under the bridge and appeared to be headed home. He decided to step on the stones sticking out of the water to get to the other side. Right in the middle, Kevin stepped on a rock that rolled downward and so did he, falling in about a foot of water. He jumped up and screamed and splashed the next few feet to the bank on the other side of the creek and ran around the corner of the bridge. When he was gone, Lucas allowed himself to laugh out loud and asked Prescott if he moved that rock in the creek.

"No, Kevin did that all by himself."

FIVE

POWER TO CHOOSE

Destiny is not subject to chance, but fashioned by the choices we make.

Lucas grabbed the golden box and headed home. As he was walking up the creek bank he looked at the Power Ring with the crystal now stuck in the center of the ring and questioned Prescott,

"I thought the Power Ring was to be used for good. Getting Kevin wet wasn't good, was it?"

Prescott replied, *"Actually it was very good if both you and Kevin can learn something from today's adventure."*

As he thought about what happened, Lucas said, "My dad always says, 'what goes around, comes around.' Maybe he learned that the way you treat others is how you will be treated."

"Sometimes what goes around does not come as quickly as it did for Kevin today, but trust me, it always comes around," said Prescott. *"What about you? What did you learn?"*

Lucas thought a moment, "I suppose I could learn to trust you."

Lucas was surprised to hear a chameleon laugh when Prescott said, "That would be a great lesson to learn!"

Lucas thought hard for some other lessons. "How about the lesson that actions have consequences."

"Excellent!" said Prescott. *"We can make a choice, but we do not get to choose the consequence. There are some laws that cannot be broken. For*

example, if someone makes the choice to jump off of a cliff, they must obey the law of gravity, and unless they have wings to fly, they will fall. The consequence is linked directly to the choice. People make choices all the time and then try to blame others for the bad consequences that follow. What they do not understand is that we do not get to choose the consequences after we make the choice."

"You need to get home now. Besides, I am ready for some more crickets."

As they neared the house, Prescott said, *"Lucas, I would like you to look up the meaning of your name. I think that you will find it very interesting."*

When Lucas got home, his mother asked, "What took you so long? Is everything all right?"

Lucas replied, "Everything is fine. I just stopped to look at some rocks under the bridge."

"Well, now that you are home, I need you to do a few things around the house. Will you please put away your things that are scattered throughout the family room and put your books on the shelves in the closet? But first, I need you to sweep the leaves and grass off of the walkway and front porch. I have some friends coming over in about thirty minutes and I do not want the leaves or grass clippings tracked into the house."

"Okay Mom," replied Lucas. He put Prescott into his cage and he went to the garage to get the broom. Lucas thought that maybe he could use the ring to move the grass away from the porch and the house toward the sidewalk. Lucas turned the pointer on the ring to the Three Arrows and thought about the grass moving toward the street. What happened next was a total surprise! Instead of moving away from the house the leaves and grass clippings started to form into a miniature whirlwind and Lucas could not control the movement of the grass. The "grassy tornado" moved around the lawn and back onto the walkway and then toward the porch.

"No, no, no, no, no!" said Lucas and then he remembered the ring and released his hold on it, and the grass and leaves just dropped to the ground, in the middle of the walkway.

Lucas heard Prescott's voice in his head, *"Are you having a little trouble sweeping the porch?"*

Lucas was not sure whether Prescott was asking a simple question or if there was a hint of sarcasm in his voice.

"What I am doing wrong?" asked Lucas.

"Lucas, who were you helping with the grass, you or your mother?"

"Well, I am helping my mother." said Lucas.

"True, you are helping your mother, but you are also trying to take a shortcut. Work is very important to building character and there are no shortcuts to character building."

"Then using the ring to clean my room would probably not work either."

"I thought that might be coming next. No, you need to clean up your room with your hands the way that normal boys clean their rooms."

"All right, I'll get the broom and sweep the normal way like everybody else."

Lucas finished sweeping up all of the grass when the first guest pulled up in front of the house, and he went inside to pick up his things from the family room. Lucas released a few crickets into Prescott's cage for which Prescott thanked Lucas.

"Lucas, you will be tempted to use the ring to help others, and that is good as long as you do not do anything that will affect the course of history."

Lucas asked, "But how will I know if my choice affects history?"

"You will need to follow your heart and listen to what your heart tells you."

"Oh, you mean like listening to my conscience?" asked Lucas.

"Yes, it is like listening to your conscience, but it is more than that." said Prescott. "This gift you are developing will speak to your mind and you will feel it in your heart. As you develop your gift and it becomes stronger, you will wonder how you can use this gift in other ways. Your heart will tell you. For example, when you thought about using the ring to clean your room, what did your heart tell you?"

"It told me that maybe I was cheating. Sometimes it feels like you are my conscience."

"I suppose it might feel that way to you but it is my responsibility to teach you. Do you want to learn to master the ring? Because if you do, you will also be learning to master yourself."

Lucas realized that Prescott was a lot older and probably wiser. He also realized that Prescott had chosen him for a reason, and he wanted to learn more about the Power Ring and his purpose with it. Lucas said, "I want to learn everything you can teach me."

"Lucas, the choices we make are dependent on the knowledge we have, and the more we know, the better our choices. Knowledge is the key to success. Along with the knowledge and power that comes with the ring, you have the responsibility to learn all you can."

"Do you mean learn all I can in school?"

"There is much you will learn in school, but there are many places you can learn by observing

and reading. Lucas, do you know the difference between knowledge and wisdom?"

Lucas thought about this for a moment and replied, "Knowledge is what you know in your head and wisdom is," Lucas hesitated to see if his heart would give him the answer as Prescott had promised, then it came to him, "knowledge is what you know in your head and wisdom is how you use that knowledge with your heart."

"That is absolutely correct! Now, how about some more crickets?"

SIX

FROZEN IN TIME

After everyone else is gone, make sure you like the person left behind.

Lucas remembered Prescott's instruction to look up the meaning of his name. After he released some crickets into Prescott's cage, Lucas got on to the Internet and looked up his name. He discovered that in several languages, the meaning of Lucas was light. He also learned that Lightfoot had its origins in England and it was the name of someone that was a speedy runner or messenger. He wondered if that meant that he was a messenger of light. Maybe it has something to do with the symbol on the ring that looked like the sun.

He then heard Prescott in his head, *"Yes, Lucas, it has everything to do with the Light Power symbol. If you are patient, I will teach you all you need to know when the time is right."*

That night after dinner, Lucas took Prescott into the back yard to practice some of the things he had been taught. He pulled the Power Ring from his pocket and turned the pointer to the Three Arrows for telekinesis and squeezed the symbol.

Prescott said, *"Now look at an object and think about where you want it to be."*

Lucas was sitting on the tire swing and looked at a plastic sand bucket sitting outside the sandbox. He began to imagine the bucket inside the sandbox and to his amazement the bucket actually started moving! Lucas got so excited that he lost his concentration and the bucket banged into the side of the sandbox.

"Wow! Did you see that? That was so cool!"

"Yes, Lucas, that was cool. Now try it again, and this time concentrate on putting it inside the sandbox."

Lucas tried a few more times until he was successful.

"*Very good,*" said Prescott, "*now try something a little larger.*"

Lucas noticed that the wooden steps up to the trampoline had fallen over. He concentrated on lifting the steps back into place and was able to move them upright after dropping them a few times.

"*Excellent,*" said Prescott. "*Now I would like you to practice moving many things at once. They are light, but there are many pine needles on the trampoline. I want you to move all of them at once. Do not think of them as many objects but just one. Move them as if there were a gust of wind.*"

Lucas concentrated a little longer and a little harder, and within a few moments all of the needles blew off the trampoline.

Prescott asked, "*How did you do that so quickly?*"

"Well," said Lucas, "I took your idea, but instead of moving the needles, I thought about moving the air across the surface so that the wind would do the work."

Prescott said, *"You are indeed a fast learner. You have learned to use the elements around you to accomplish your goal. Remember what you have learned this day. The time will come when you will need to use the things that you find in nature for your safety."*

Lucas asked, "Can I practice being invisible?" Prescott agreed, and Lucas turned the pointer to the Double-S and squeezed. He felt the ring vibrate slightly and he realized he didn't know what to do next. He heard Prescott in his head,

"Imagine that there is a curtain between you and everyone else all around you."

There was no one else in the back yard so he just imagined a curtain surrounding him and his little brother coming out of the back door. To his amazement, the screen door opened and his little brother Gavin stepped out and yelled, "Lucas, Mom wants you to come in!"

Gavin saw that the swing was moving and thought that Lucas must have just gotten off so he came closer to look around the side of the house. Lucas was still on the swing as Gavin walked by but he could not see Lucas. Gavin called out again with no response so he went back into the house.

Lucas let go of the ring and put it back into his pocket. Just as he got to the screen door, his mom opened it.

"Oh, there you are. Gavin said he could not find you."

"I was hiding and playing my invisibility game," said Lucas, "but I came when I heard him call me." His mom just shook her head as Lucas came in the house.

It had been another eventful day and Lucas had learned much from Prescott. He was glad it was Friday and he would not have to see Kevin until Monday at school. The next two days Lucas practiced the things he had learned from Prescott. Lucas was determined that he was never going to let Kevin scare him again.

On Saturday morning, Lucas asked if he could ride his bike over to his cousin's house a few streets away. His mom agreed but he was to have Aunt Lisa call her when he got there. Lucas decided to take the shortcut to his cousin's house which was across the footpath bridge where he had encountered Kevin earlier. He did not expect to see Kevin, but he was wrong. Before he crossed the bridge, he stopped, and saw Kevin on the other side tossing a Frisbee to his dog in his front yard. Lucas guessed that Kevin lived in that house near the bridge. Lucas thought about going the long way around, out to the busy street and then back to his cousin's house but remembered his resolve not to be afraid of Kevin. Lucas had learned from Prescott about the Ring's power for stopping time so Lucas turned the pointer to the Double-T with the Sun and held it in his hand.

As Lucas rode his bike over the bridge, he squeezed the Double-T. Kevin had his back to Lucas and had just thrown the Frisbee. The dog was in mid-air about to bite down on the Frisbee when everything stopped moving except Lucas. Kevin froze with his arm stretched out, his dog froze in mid-air, and everything got very quiet. It was so quiet that Lucas could not even hear the wind in his ears. Lucas rode on the sidewalk several feet from where Kevin was standing. When he was far enough down the street, Lucas stopped, turned around, and was watching Kevin when he stopped squeezing the ring. It was kind of funny to see Kevin and his dog frozen in time and then to see them moving again as if nothing had happened. Lucas just smiled and kept on riding to his cousin's house.

SEVEN

BULLY BENDING

That which you send into the life of others will come back into your own.

Kevin Cherno had moved to the area about two years ago and quickly made a reputation for himself at school. He would be devious and do things to the other students that he could easily deny, and then make sure they saw him grinning as they discovered what he had done. Last month Kevin let the air out of Lucas's tires and he had to walk his bike home. Kevin rode past and said, "What's the matter Lucas, are you feeling a little deflated?" And then he laughed. It was just the way he was laughing that Lucas knew that Kevin was the one that had let the air out.

Lucas felt a combination of apprehension and excitement as he got ready for school on Monday morning. He remembered the fear he felt under the bridge as Kevin was looking for him. He also remembered something that Prescott had told him on the walk back from the creek.

Prescott had said, *"When you fear someone, one way to change that feeling is to imagine that person with big mouse ears, a long mouse tail and a squeaky mouse voice. And then in your mind, you shrink them down to the size of a small little mouse."*

Lucas had tried that and surprisingly he began smiling as he thought about Kevin. Lucas practiced that several times over the weekend and again as he was going to school. This time he felt a little less nervous about seeing Kevin at school.

When Lucas got to his classroom, he sat down next to Hailey and said, "Good morning."

She smiled back, "Hi Lucas. How was your weekend?"

Lucas thought about all of the excitement and the things that he learned, but remembering his promise, he just replied, "It was good."

He looked past Hailey as Kevin sat down. Kevin looked over at Lucas and gave him an angry stare. Lucas started feeling the same fear he had felt at the creek and then remembered what Prescott had taught him and he started to laugh as he looked away from Kevin and down at his desk.

Hailey asked him, "What are you laughing about?"

"Oh, it's nothing. I was just thinking about some big mouse ears."

The bell range and Miss Harrison stood up and said, "Good morning, class. It's time to share your homework assignment with the rest of the class." There were a few audible groans.

Lucas's class had been studying poetry, and Miss Harrison had given the assignment to the class to write a poem that had a special meaning in their lives. There was quite a variety of topics from the students. Hailey had spoken about friends, Kevin had a short poem about his dog, and Sarah read her poem about spending time at the beach with her family. When it came time for Lucas Lightfoot, he went to the front of the class and said,

"I met a new friend in my neighborhood and he has taught me some very important lessons. This poem is about one of those lessons. The name of my poem is *The Boomerang*."

Life is like a boomerang,
I know that this is true.
That which you send to the lives of others
Will always come back to you.

It matters not how big the arc
Or how long it flies,
For surely as the sun comes up,
It will hit you with surprise.

Listen closely to this advice,
It's what we all must do.
Send out friendship and words of kindness,
And they will come back to you.

Lucas had meant this poem mostly for Kevin, but Miss Harrison said that it was a good reminder of the Golden Rule.

At the beginning of lunch, Lucas was walking by Kevin as he

was getting a drink at the drinking fountain. Kevin looked up and ran his hand through the stream of water and splashed water on to Lucas.

Kevin said," I missed you at the creek."

"What do you mean?" questioned Lucas.

"I saw you go down at the creek, but then you disappeared."

"I disappeared? That sounds like magic." said Lucas with a smile.

He could see that Kevin was getting mad and thought that maybe he needed to cool off. He remembered what Prescott had taught him about stopping time, and using his mind, Lucas turned the pointer on the Power Ring in his pocket to the Double-T symbol and imagined squeezing the ring. Everyone around Lucas slowed to a stop, and it got very quiet.

Lucas walked up to Kevin and turned him around so he was facing the drinking fountain. He "helped" Kevin bend his head down toward the water fountain and then put his hand on the faucet handle. Lucas walked to the corner of the building and thought, *"What goes around comes around."* Lucas let go of the ring, and the weight of Kevin's hand turned on the water and soaked his head! He heard Kevin yelling and saw the surprised look on Kevin's face as he tried to remember why he was getting his head drenched! Lucas was hoping that Kevin would learn that choosing to treat others unkindly would only result in unwanted consequences.

EIGHT

LUNCH TIME HERO

Exercise your courage everyday. You might surprise yourself to know how much you have.

Lucas took his lunch to the soccer field to be alone and think. As he sat down on the cool grass, he heard a siren in the distance. That sound took him back a couple of years to when he and his dad had driven to the foothills to see a fire. Lucas thought it was kind of pretty to see the red glow on the hills at dusk, and the setting sun was a deep red from the smoke in the air. All of a sudden, the wind shifted and the smoke and the fire started coming down the hill towards them. His dad was calm and started the truck to drive away, but Lucas was truly scared.

That night at home, Lucas had heard that his uncle, who was a fireman, was caught on a ridge with his fire crew. The wind had shifted on them and they were trapped with fire all around.

They only had a few seconds to get into their fire shelters before the fire raced over them. One of the six-man crew did not survive, and Lucas remembered the funeral where he had seen the fireman's wife and children crying.

Every time he heard a siren from a fire truck, this memory came back to him and only intensified his fear of fire and being burned. The bell to end lunch brought him back to the present, and he started to walk back to class.

Lucas saw Hailey walking back from the outdoor lunch tables. She was reading a book and she had her earphones in her ears. What she didn't see was a garbage truck backing up. She didn't hear the loud reverse beeping of the truck, and Lucas was sure she would not hear him yelling at her to stop. He had to act quickly. He immediately thought about the pointer on the ring moving to the Double-T and squeezed the ring desperately. The shadow of the huge truck had just crossed Hailey's path and she looked up in horror when everything slowed to a stop except for Lucas. He ran over to Hailey, grabbed her hand and pulled her to safety. They were up on the sidewalk when Lucas let go of the ring, the noise level increased, and the world around Lucas started moving again.

He was still holding Hailey's hand when she remembered the impending danger. The adrenaline was flowing through her veins. When she realized she was safe, she grabbed him with both arms and gave him a hug of gratitude.

"Thank you!" she said. She was still shaking when she asked, "How did you do that? How did you save me from being run over by the trash truck?"

Lucas just smiled and said, "Sometimes we just react without fear to save others in danger. Besides," he said with a smile, "I just stopped time and moved you out of the way."

Hailey figured that she was not going to get an answer she could believe or understand, so she said, "Well, however you did it, thank you very much."

"Hailey," Lucas said with a serious face, "can we keep this our secret? I don't want anyone to make a big deal out of this."

"Okay," she replied as she gave his hand a squeeze. "It's our secret."

That night at home, Lucas's mother got a phone call, but he did not pay any attention until he heard his mom say, "Yes, he is in Miss Harrison's class." Then he heard his mom say, "Well, that is not too surprising. Lucas has always been a helpful boy."

Lucas thought, *"Oh great! Hailey told her mom!"*

They talked more on the phone about school, teachers, children, and other things that were not interesting to Lucas.

After she hung up, she came into Lucas's room and said, "Hailey Sinclair's mother called to thank you for saving Hailey's life."

"What did she say?" asked Lucas.

"She said that Hailey was about to step into a driveway with a garbage truck backing out and you stopped her. Is that what happened?" asked his mom.

"Yep, that's about right," replied Lucas.

He was glad that Hailey did not say exactly what happened, but then again, she wasn't too sure herself. Lucas liked being able to have a secret with Hailey.

NINE

RANGER, THE TALKING DOG

*Your dog may admire you, but that is not proof
that you are a wonderful person.*

It didn't take long for the news to get around school that Lucas had saved Hailey, and Miss Harrison made a point of thanking him in class. After school, Lucas stayed behind until all of the others had left.

"Miss Harrison," said Lucas, "I was kind of embarrassed today. I told Hailey that I didn't want to make a big deal out of it."

"I'm sorry, Lucas, I had no idea."

"That's okay. I wanted to talk about something else."

"What is it?" asked Miss Harrison.

"Kevin Cherno is sometimes a bully and he doesn't like me very much."

"Has he done anything to hurt you?" asked Miss Harrison.

"Well, he has splashed water on me, and I have seen him push Trevor. He has also tripped some boys in the other class and made it look like an accident. Miss Harrison, why does he do things like that?"

"That is a tough question to answer. There may be several reasons," said Miss Harrison. "Most often they learn that behavior at home either from parents or an older brother or sister or from their peers. The bully is often someone that needs to be in control. Sometimes it is because they do not feel love from others, and maybe it is their way of getting attention. I know that Kevin's parents are divorced and he lives with his mother and older brother. We don't know all the reasons why someone is a bully, but it could be that they are angry about something, and it is usually connected to how a person feels about oneself."

Miss Harrison looked at Lucas and asked, "Are you afraid that he might hurt you?"

"Oh no," said Lucas, "I used to be afraid of him, but not anymore and I am sure he will not hurt me. I am just concerned that he might hurt himself."

Miss Harrison was quite surprised at Lucas's response. She had noticed a change in Lucas over the past few weeks. He seemed more confident and even a little more mature. Miss Harrison said, "Sometimes when a person is hurt, he wants to hurt back. A mature person will stop and try to figure out why that person is trying to hurt them. If you are concerned about helping Kevin, I would suggest that you find out what he likes or what he is good at and give him some honest complements. He might resist a little at first, but I am sure that he will appreciate your interest even if he doesn't show it."

To help Lucas feel more at ease, Miss Harrison said, "I will watch the situation in class and on the school grounds to see if there is anything I need to do to help. And if necessary, I will send a note home to Kevin's mother."

Lucas thanked Miss Harrison and headed home. Yes, the word was getting around school that Lucas Lightfoot was being called the "Lunch Time Hero."

As Lucas was nearing his house, he saw a dog chasing a cat across a lawn toward the street. He also saw a car on a collision course with the cat and the dog. He thought quickly to determine if he could use any of the symbols on the ring to stop the dog. He used the telekinetic power to turn the pointer to the Three Arrows and then quickly slid a trash can that was at the curb in front of the dog so he would either stop or run into it. The dog let out a loud yelp when he ran into the can which saved him from running into the street and being hit by the car. The car had to swerve to miss the cat so both dog and cat were safe.

Lucas ran to the dog just as it was getting up. He kneeled down and let the dog smell the back of his hand and then began stroking the dog's head. The dog had a collar so maybe it would have a tag with the name and address of the owner. The dog looked familiar and the tag showed that the dog's name was Ranger.

"Oh great!" said Lucas out loud, "I just saved Kevin Cherno's dog!"

Lucas thought this might be an opportunity to change Kevin's attitude toward him so he headed home. He held onto Ranger's collar and walked the one block to his house.

When Lucas got home he told his mom that he stopped Kevin's dog from chasing a cat into the street and from getting run over by a car. He asked if he could take the dog to Kevin's house and explain how he found him.

His mom said, "Isn't that the boy who's not very nice to you?"

"I talked with Miss Harrison about Kevin, and she thinks that he may be a bully because he's angry at something or maybe someone in his family was a bully to him. If I take his dog home and explain how I found him, maybe he won't be mean to me anymore."

"Where does he live?" asked his mother.

"A couple of houses past the footpath bridge," replied Lucas.

"Okay, but be careful and come right home, we have to go to the store before your dad comes home from work." said his mom.

Lucas ran to get Prescott and the mesh pack and then untied Ranger from the garden hose. That was the only thing he could find to prevent him from running in the street again.

As they walked toward Kevin's house, Lucas heard Prescott ask,

"So, Ranger, why are you limping?"

Lucas was surprised that Prescott was talking with Ranger but even more surprised to hear the dog's response.

"I was chasing a cat and this big green thing moved right in my way and I smashed my nose and hurt my paw. Then this nice person took me to a new house and tied me up. It looks like we are going to my master's home now."

"Yes, we are going to your home," said Prescott. "My keeper is a fine young man, and it is my duty to protect him and you should too."

"I will protect him, too." said Ranger.

As Lucas walked up to the front porch, the door swung open and Kevin came out and said, "What are you doing with my dog?"

Before Lucas could answer, Ranger ran to Kevin and jumped up on him and ran back to Lucas and jumped on him and licked his face and then back to Kevin. That seemed to calm Kevin, and Lucas explained that he stopped Ranger from chasing a cat into the street in front of a moving car. Lucas was careful to leave out the part about moving the trash can. Kevin had been ready to get angry at Lucas, but all he said was, "Oh. Okay. Thanks."

Lucas asked, "What kind of dog is Ranger?"

Kevin replied, "Ranger is a Border Collie and I got him from my dad on my eighth birthday."

"Does he do any tricks?" asked Lucas.

"Sure," said Kevin, "watch this."

Kevin picked up a Frisbee on the porch and slapped it against his leg and called to

Ranger. Ranger lowered his head down with his rear up in the air and barked once, waiting for Kevin to toss the Frisbee. He tossed it slowly and Ranger ran after it and jumped about three feet in the air and grabbed it in his teeth. Lucas had seen that before and had even seen Ranger floating in mid air but he still said how cool Ranger was to catch the Frisbee. Lucas had been thinking about his conversation with Miss Harrison and asked Kevin a question.

"Kevin, sometimes you act like a bully and I was wondering if you know why."

Kevin was surprised at the question and started to get angry but remembered that Lucas had gone out of his way to save Ranger and softened his response.

"I don't know. Maybe I am just trying to get some attention, to get noticed."

Lucas asked, "Do you think that the attention of bothering or hurting others is good attention?"

"No, probably not," answered Kevin.

"If you want some attention, how about we start tossing a Frisbee during recess? And maybe we can work together on the book report assignment."

Kevin said, "That would be good. I would like that."

After a few minutes, Lucas remembered that he had told his mom he would be right home and said, "Kevin, I have to go home. My mom is waiting for me to go to the store."

"Okay. Hey! Thanks again for bringing Ranger home."

As Lucas turned to go, Prescott said, *"I do not think that you will have any more trouble from Kevin."*

TEN

THE RESCUE

You will never know how strong you are until being strong is your only choice.

Things had been a lot different over the last few weeks at school between Lucas and Kevin. Although they did not become friends, there was a quiet truce between them. Kevin did not bother Lucas, and they even found they had a few things in common. They worked together and they each got an A on the book report assignment.

One evening as Lucas turned out the light and climbed into bed, Prescott asked, *"Have you been listening to your heart?"*

"I think so." replied Lucas. "When I saved Hailey and Ranger a few weeks ago, I made some really quick decisions but I think my heart helped me decide. And that time at the drinking fountain, my heart wanted Kevin to learn that people should be treated with kindness and not be bullied."

Lucas asked, "What about the other symbols on the ring? When will you teach me about those?"

"All in good time my eager young friend. You have been one of my brightest students, and you will accomplish great things in your life. But for now, be patient. There are a few more lessons to learn."

"What lessons?" asked Lucas.

"You will know them when you learn them. Now go to sleep."

Lucas looked forward to next week at school. He was the classroom "Student of the Week." During his turn as student of the week, he had certain classroom privileges, as well as share day. He was most eager about share day. He wanted to bring Prescott to school. Lucas had arranged with Miss Harrison to bring Prescott to class on Thursday that week. The day arrived and Lucas told the class how he found Prescott on the sidewalk in front of his house and about the kind woman that let Lucas keep the chameleon. Lucas told the class how chameleons eat and had brought some crickets to school to show the class. Several of the students wanted to hold Prescott, and Lucas was considering it. Then he heard Prescott.

"That is not a good idea, Lucas. It is time to put me back in the cage."

Lucas decided to have some fun with the class and pretended to have a conversation with Prescott.

"What's that, Prescott? Did you say to put you back in the cage to eat the crickets?"

Lucas turned to the class and said, "Prescott just told me that he's hungry and wants to go back in the cage to get the crickets." The class erupted with giggles. As Lucas placed Prescott back into his cage, the entire class watched with wide eyes as Prescott methodically snatched up crickets using his tongue. There was a lot of commotion from the children because they all

wanted a close look at Prescott eating the crickets.
After Prescott had grabbed the last cricket, Miss
Harrison saw that it was time to head out to the
garden.

Thursday was the day that Miss Harrison's
class worked in the school garden. Each class was
responsible for a portion of the garden, and they
all wanted their portion of the garden to do well.
There were other schools in the area that had
gardens, but Lucas's school had an award-
winning-garden. Miss Harrison's class was
responsible for the sunflowers and the carrots.
Half of the class worked on weeding around the
carrots and the other half were working on the
sunflowers.

They had planted the tall variety of
sunflowers and Lucas's group was putting some
bamboo stakes near each plant to support the
heavy blossom.

That's when they heard the fire alarm. Miss
Harrison had helped the class through several fire
drills, but they usually knew when they were
coming. This might be the real thing. It had been
a warm May and the dry desert winds were
starting early. In Southern California it is common

to have wild fires in the hills, but to have one this early in the year was different. Lucas remembered his Uncle Brett telling the story of being on the ridge with the fire all around. As he thought about the fireman that died and his family, an overwhelming fear enveloped him. Lucas was thinking about his uncle when someone from the school office ran out to the garden.

"Miss Harrison! Miss Harrison! This is not a drill and you need to get all of the children to the far corner of the soccer field."

Lucas thought that he could hear the sirens in the distance and he saw smoke coming from the cafeteria near his classroom. He saw that some of the students were already coming out of the school buildings.

That's when he heard Prescott. *"Lucas, are you going to come get me? I am still in the classroom. Besides, there is someone else still in the building that you need to help!"*

Prescott had become Lucas's best friend in such a short time, and he wanted to go get him.

But his fear of fire was so powerful that he just froze.

Then he heard Prescott's voice again. *"Lucas, I know that you have a fear of fire, but you need to trust me."*

Every time he trusted Prescott, Lucas was able to accomplish what was needed. In spite of his fear, Lucas knew what he needed to do. Asking Miss Harrison if he could get Prescott would be met with opposition so he went off by himself and ducked behind some bushes. He wasn't sure if he should try to stop time or be invisible. He chose to let the firemen do their job because he did not know how big of an area would be affected by stopping time. He turned the ring to the Double-S and squeezed hard and imagined a curtain surrounding him and hiding him from others.

He was now invisible and started running back to the class as everyone else was walking toward the field. He had to run around the students so they wouldn't bump into him.

Everyone else was walking away from the danger and Lucas was running right into it.

He got to his classroom and found the door had been locked and he could not get inside. He ran around to the other side with the windows hoping one would be open but they were all locked as well. His eyes started to burn as the wind was blowing the smoke between the buildings and he started to cough. He had to get Prescott! He quickly turned the ring to the Three Arrows and looked at the window lock and willed it open.

He could hear Prescott in his head say, *"It's about time! I was getting just a little concerned that something might have happened to you. We need to hurry!"*

The window was hinged at the top and Lucas pulled it open and up with just enough room to pull himself up and squeeze through. He ran to the counter at the back of the room and pulled Prescott from the cage and slid him into his shoulder pack. As he ran for the door, he heard a voice in his head, but it wasn't Prescott's voice this time. It was his Uncle Brett. He remembered him saying that if the door is hot, do not open it. As he neared the door he could feel some heat and wondered how the fire had gotten there so quickly. He turned around to head for the windows and saw that the bushes between the buildings had also caught fire. Just then the fire sprinklers came on and Lucas was soaked within a few seconds. Again he heard Uncle Brett's voice telling him to look for all possible escape routes, and Lucas remembered that there were doors between the class rooms and ran toward the First and Second Grade class rooms. Once he was through one room, he ran toward the next door away from the direction of the fire. When he got to the last room, the fire alarm was directly above him.

The noise was so loud he put his hands up to cover his ears. As he did, he tilted his head toward the ground and he saw a girl sitting on the floor crying.

Lucas rushed over to her, and in a loud voice, asked, "What are you still doing here?"

She said, "I went to the bathroom, and when I came out everyone was gone. I didn't know what to do or where to go."

"What is your name?"

"Anna," she replied.

"Well, Anna, you are going to be safe." Lucas wasn't sure of that himself but he needed to be strong for little Anna.

Lucas took her by the hand and said, "We have to get out of here!"

They ran for the door, and Lucas felt for any heat. There was none so he opened it slowly. He had gone far enough from the fire and saw water coming over the top of the building that was directed at the flames. Lucas knew that the firemen had arrived and that they were doing their job. Lucas opened the door all the way, and they turned away from the fire to run but he had forgotten that there was an eight foot chain-link fence. It was meant to keep vandals out, but now it was trapping them. He thought about putting Anna on his back and climbing since she was too little to climb by herself.

"Prescott, can you help us?"

"Who is Prescott," asked Anna.

He didn't answer.

Lucas heard Prescott in his head say, *"You have all the power you need in the ring. Just trust yourself."*

Lucas thought to himself, *"Being invisible won't get us over the fence and even if I stopped time, we still have to climb. How do I use telekinesis to get us over?"*

Lucas could feel the heat from the fire, and he could feel his own fear rising, causing his muscles to lock and his mind to go blank. He was frozen in fear and stood motionless as he stared at the fence until he heard Anna's voice.

"Are we going to die?" That brought Lucas out of his stupor. He shook his head hard to break himself out of the feeling of being powerless.

"No! We are not going to die! We are going to get out of here."

Lucas knew that the firemen might be coming around the building soon, and he did not want to hang around to see them or be seen by anyone else. Lucas had been able to move other

96

objects but how could he move himself and Anna? Lucas decided to follow Prescott's advice and trust himself. He had to try something new, and an idea started to take shape in his mind. He turned the ring to the Three Arrows. Lucas was about a foot taller than Anna and as he looked down at her and said,

"I am going to get us out of here but you have to trust me and do exactly what I tell you."

"All right," replied Anna. Lucas could see the fear in her eyes that were still wet with tears.

Lucas said, "Anna, I want you to wrap your arms around me very tight. Put your face against my shirt, stand on my feet, and close your eyes as tight as you can."

She followed his instructions and Lucas wrapped his arms around Anna. Then, using the power of telekinesis, Lucas imagined them rising in the air and floating over the fence. The faith that Lucas had in his ability was rewarded with what was an amazing scene. Lucas, Anna, and Prescott rose slowly to the height of the building and floated about fifteen feet past the fence and then descended slowly to the ground. Lucas was glad there was no one around to see them. Once they were on the ground, Lucas released his grip on Anna and he said,

"You can open your eyes now. We need to hurry and run to the back soccer field area."

Anna's teacher was frantic when she discovered that one of her students was missing. Two firefighters got the assignment to search for Anna. They were coming toward the school when they saw Lucas and Anna come running around the building toward them. One of the firemen picked up Anna and carried her over to her teacher. Lucas walked along beside him and then turned to join his class. Miss Harrison watched Lucas and the fireman carrying Anna and was thinking about what she was going to say to Lucas for not following directions during this emergency and wandering off away from the class.

As Lucas joined his class, Miss Harrison put her arm around his shoulder and walked a short distance from her class. Miss Harrison saw the shoulder pack on Lucas and knew that he went back to the classroom.

"Lucas, you were supposed to stay with the class. Do you realize how dangerous it was to go back for your chameleon?"

"Miss Harrison, I am so sorry that I left the class, but I had to save Prescott. He is very special to me and I needed to go back to get him."

"When I was leaving I heard someone crying and found Anna in her classroom. I knew that I couldn't wait for the firemen and had to get her safely out of the building."

Miss Harrison was glad that Anna and Lucas were safe. She had taught a lot of children but never anyone like Lucas and decided that there must be something very extraordinary about Lucas and his chameleon. Her heart was softened, and she thanked Lucas again for saving Anna.

"Please stay with our class until your mother comes and you are released to go home."

Lucas stepped a few feet away from the class where he could be alone with Prescott. He found a stick and pulled Prescott out of the shoulder pack and allowed him to climb onto the stick.

Lucas looked at Prescott and said, "Your collar has the same symbols that are on the Power Ring. Do you have the same power on your collar that is on the ring?"

"I do indeed."

"Then could you have saved yourself?"

"Yes, I could have saved myself, and I could have saved little Anna. But you needed to find out for yourself what you were capable of doing. Lucas, you will never know how strong you are until being strong is the only choice you have."

"Was this a test?" asked Lucas.

"Yes, Lucas, it was. You needed to learn for yourself just how strong you are. Do you remember asking about what lessons you needed to learn before I teach you more about the Power Ring? This was one of those lessons. You have proven to me and to yourself how you will use the power you have been given. You also showed your true character by what you were willing to do. I am very pleased with your actions today."

"Thank you," replied Lucas.

Hailey Sinclair lived behind the school, and her mother ran over to pick her up and got permission from Miss Harrison to take her home. Hailey was home and watching the fire from her back yard when she saw Lucas and a little girl floating through the air and over the fence. She remembered the day that Lucas saved her from being run over by the trash truck and he had told her he had stopped time. She thought he was just being silly, but what she saw today was something that was impossible. She was determined to find out what was going on with Lucas and what secrets he might be keeping.

Because of the fire and the fact that there was only one week of school left, the district ended the school year and sent the kids home for the summer. The next day, Hailey asked if she could go to Lucas's house to talk about the fire. Her mom agreed, and Hailey called Lucas to see if she could come over.

Lucas and Hailey were in his backyard that afternoon, hanging out on the tire swing talking about the school fire, getting out of school early, and what they had planned for the summer. Things got quiet, and that's when Hailey said, "I saw you yesterday during the fire. I saw you help the little girl."

"Well I just did what anyone would do," replied Lucas.

"No. I mean I saw you holding the little girl and floating over the fence."

"I don't know what you are talking about!" protested Lucas.

"Lucas, when you saved me from the trash truck, you said that you just stopped time and I thought you were joking. I saw you and the little girl lift off of the ground, float over the fence and then after you came down, you started running around the building to the field. I was not in the soccer field. I was at home looking over my fence and I saw you. So tell me, how did you do that?"

"I guess some of the invisible angels picked us up and carried us over."

"Lucas Lightfoot, I'm serious! Tell me how you did that."

Then with a smirk, Hailey teased, "I just may have to tell everyone that I saw you and Anna float over the fence."

"And who is going to believe you? I will just say that I carried Anna on my back and I climbed over the fence," said Lucas with a grin.

Hailey groaned with frustration and asked, "Why won't you tell me?"

Lucas thought for a moment and listened to his heart. He then heard Prescott in his head.

"Lucas, you trusted yourself yesterday and what you did was very heroic. Tell Hailey that you have been granted some special powers because of your honest heart. Tell her that you will tell her the secret if she can promise that she, too, will have an honest heart and keep the secret between just the two of you."

"Well?" said Hailey. "Are you going to tell me?"

"Hailey," began Lucas, "I suppose because of my honest heart, I have been granted a gift of some special powers that are unlike anything I could have ever imagined. I can tell you about them only if you promise to keep everything I tell you a secret between us."

"I can keep a secret," said Hailey.

Lucas said, "I thought that the garbage truck incident was going to be our secret."

"I promise that I did not say a word," pleaded Hailey. "Emily Parker overheard our conversation after you saved me and she told Miss Harrison. Miss Harrison called and talked to my mom and it grew from there."

With a solemn tone, Lucas said, "The secret I have can only be used for good and to help others. You have to understand that if the wrong people find out, I may lose my ability or that it can be taken away. Or worse yet, the gift might be stolen from me."

Hailey could see the intense worry on his face, and she could hear the seriousness in his voice when Lucas said he was afraid of losing what he called "the gift".

"Lucas, I make you a solemn promise that I can be trusted to keep your secret if it means you will be safe."

"Pinky swear?"

"Pinky swear," said Hailey as they hooked little fingers together.

"All right, I will tell you, but not here and not now. We are going to visit my grandparents this weekend for my grandpa's birthday. When I get back, we can get together. and I will tell you the entire story."

From the author:

I hope you had fun reading *Lucas Lightfoot and the Fire Crystal*. In book one, Lucas finds the Power Ring with eight symbols and he learns to use the power of Telekinesis, Stopping Time, and Invisibility. A fourth symbol is mentioned without details. There are four other symbols and powers for Lucas to use. I have plans for three symbols, and I would like to hear what power, you, the reader, thinks that Lucas should have. I know that you are smart and imaginative, and I would like to have a contest. I would like to have your best ideas for a new power for Lucas. If we select your power, you will get a signed copy of book two and, with your permission and your parent's permission, I will include you by name as a character in the second book in the *Lucas Lightfoot* trilogy to be released in the summer of 2014. I will accept suggestions until February 28, 2014. After that date, the winner will be selected and your name will appear in the next book. If there are duplicates of the power selected, the winner will be chosen by the earliest date of submission. If you are under 13 years old, you must have a parent's permission to enter the contest. My grandson and I will have the final choice in the power selected. I look forward to hearing from you.

To submit your suggestion for Lucas's power, go to: www.lucaslightfoot.com and click on the POWER button.

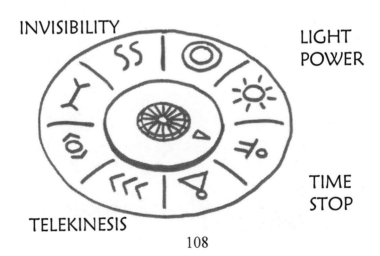

INVISIBILITY

LIGHT POWER

TIME STOP

TELEKINESIS

About the Authors

Hugo Haselhuhn lives in San Luis Obispo County and has a passion to create a positive influence for good in the lives of others. Hugo has incorporated lessons to strengthen human relations shared in this story and the readers are learning through the eyes and experiences of the characters.

This book began as a request from his co-author, eight-year-old grandson, Luke Cowdell, who wanted help in writing a "chapter book". Luke is an avid reader with an active imagination. He is also a deep thinker and asks questions seemingly beyond his years.

25138328R10064

Made in the USA
Charleston, SC
21 December 2013